Can You Fix My Heart?

This book is to help children learn how to cope with grief and give them a voice when someone they loved died from gun violence.

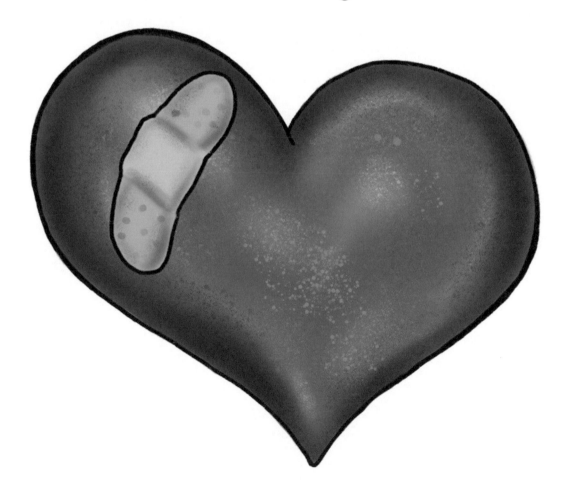

Written by

Rochelle Yates-Whittington

Illustrated by Stephanie Richardson & Travese Thomas

To order additional copies of this book, contact:
Xlibris
844-714-8691
www.Xlibris.com
Orders@Xlibris.com

ISBN: Softcover   979-8-3694-1409-5
         EBook   979-8-3694-1410-1

Library of Congress Control Number: 2023924632

Print information available on the last page

Rev. date: 01/18/2024

Dedication

This book was written in the memory of my 5-year-old son, Marcus Yates who was murdered July 18, 1988. It is also dedicated to Marcus' brothers, Malcolm Yates who was shot twice at the age of 6 and Anthony Yates who relentlessly tried to save Marcus' life at the age of 11 years old. Nine months after Marcus' death his baby sister Tanisha Yates was born.

My hope for writing this book is that it will help give children a voice everywhere who suffered the loss of a loved one, but especially from gun violence. Also, to let them know that the hearts of those who commits heinous acts of violence lacks conscience or compassion for human life. In addition, we should respect each other's right to live and to not worry about being killed by those hiding their pain behind a gun.

My prayer is that one day that we as human beings will do what the Bible says in Matthew 22:37-39: You should love the Lord thy God with all your heart, with all your soul, and with all your mind. This is the first and great commandment. And the second is like unto it; You should love thy neighbor as yourself.

To my husband, Pastor Bryan Whittington, thank you for your support by providing me a safe environment that allowed God to help me write this book for hurting children.

To my friends and family, thank you for being there for me during the hardest times of my life.

To my late
Aunt Opheila Smith, who continually prayed for me and loved me unconditionally from the very beginning.

Mommy, can you stop my heart from hurting said Kevin. Mom held Kevin close and hugged him.

Mommy, why did those bad people hurt my daddy?

Sweetheart, there are people in
the world who do bad things.

Their hearts are stuck in a
dark box and can't get out.

Kevin, I will take you to
see someone who can
help fix your heart.

Mommy, how can they fix it?
Will they put a band aid on it?

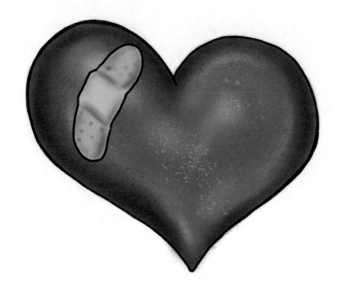

They will talk to you until your
heart feels a little better.

Kevin, stop saying it's your fault, because it's not your fault what happened to your dad. Those bad people hurt your dad. It's their fault.

I just wish I was there to help him, said Kevin.

Mommy! sometimes I can't sleep,
because I miss daddy so much.

Kevin, when you find yourself not able to sleep, talk to God about what makes your heart feels sad. God hears your prayers and He will make your heart feel better.

Mommy, can you come to my school and tell my teachers that my heart feels sad sometimes.

Some of the kids tease me and call me a cry baby when they see tears coming out my eyes.

I don't want to cry, but the tears keep coming out on their own when I think about daddy.

Kevin, everyone cries when they feel really sad or hurt. It's okay to cry.

Kevin, one day you will feel better; just know that I love you and your daddy loved you too.

Mommy, do you cry and does your heart hurt too?

Yes, Kevin, my heart hurts sometimes too, but you can always come to me when you want to talk. We can pray together to ask God for help.

Daddy, would not want us to be sad for a long time. He would want us to be happy again.

Mommy, my heart feels
better when we pray and
talk about daddy.

Yes, Kevin, praying and talking
about what bothers us is
better than keeping it inside.

I love you Mommy.

I love you too Kevin.

The End

How does your heart feel today?

Happy

Inside a dark box

Coming out the dark box

Sad

Reviews (2019)

Paige Jenkins, 9 years old: "I liked the book, because Kevin's mom was there to support him. She went to the school to talk to his teacher, because some of the kids were teasing him. Kevin's mom took him to see a doctor who could fix his heart. When Kevin talked to his mom and the doctor his heart started to feel better".

Jaylen Yates, 7 years old: "I liked when Kevin talk to his dad at night."

Renee Whittington, 13 years old: "There are a lot of kids who are like Kevin and I am glad that Kevin had someone to talk to."

Quincy Cruz, 8 years old: "When they talk about dad it makes Kevin feel better."

Marcus Yates, 6 years old: "When you talk to mom your heart comes out the box."

Taylor Yates, 11 years old: I like that they talked and mom was strong enough to keep the conversation going."

Camille Yates, 4 years old: "I loved it. I like when the heart came out the box."

Mari Fields-Yates, 16 years old: Talking things out can fix any problem."

About the Author

Rochelle Yates-Whittington, mother of Marcus J. Yates, the 5-year old child who was gunned down inside a candy store in Southwest Philadelphia on July 18, 1988. She is the wife and the assistant to Pastor Bryan Whittington of Christ Covenant Family Worship Center, in Delaware. She is a mother of seven; Anthony, Malcolm, Marcus, Tanisha, Myleka, Shanice, and Renee, adopted mother of two, step-mother of one, grandmother of 12, and foster mother/Godmother to countless others.

Product of Overbook High School in West Philadelphia, Rochelle then graduated from Community College and Eastern University with her Bachelor's in Organizational Management and AA Early Childhood Education. She was employed by the Children Hospital of Philadelphia as an Infant Toddler Specialist. For many years she worked with at-risk children and families, helping to provide a better life for those in her community. In addition to being fully employed, Rochelle marched, protested against gun violence, and spoke to students at numerous elementary, middle, high schools and colleges in Philadelphia about the importance of making good choices.

Rochelle travelled to Harrisburg, PA and Washington, DC to stand with the Governor and Legislators, as an activist seeking federal support of common sense gun laws to stop the violence that plagues the city which she loves.

Rochelle received numerous awards for her work in fighting against violence in the city of Philadelphia. Rochelle has been recognized by President G.W. Bush, Governor Bob Casey, Governor Tom Ridge, Congressman Lucien Blackwell, U.S. Senator Harris Wofford, State Senator Anthony Hardy Williams, Mayor Wilson Goode, Mayor Ed Rendell and Mayor Michael Nutter.

Continuing the movement, Rochelle was a guest on nationally syndicated television shows such as; the Montel Williams Show, Joan Rivers Show, and the Geraldo Rivera Show.

Rochelle, has been the recipient of the WCAU Channel 10 Spirit of Philadelphia Award, Liberty Bell Award presented by Mayor Goode, Rich Montgomery Hero of Peace Award, Women of Excellence Award, and recently Mother of the Movement Award for her work in bringing attention to the violence that has caused so many innocent lives to be lost. Former City Councilwoman Jannie Blackwell dedicated a "tree of life" a Memorial of Marcus J. Yates, at Lewis C. Cassidy Elementary School, the school he once attended. The tree of life dedication and revealing where the keynote address and ceremonial planting was performed by former Mayor Michael Nutter. In 2018, 30 years after his death, Councilman Kenyatta Johnson introduced a proclamation to City Council to rename the street where Marcus was killed from 60th and Springfield Ave to Marcus J. Yates Way, which passed posthumously.

DECEMBER 16, 2016

THWEST GLOBE TIMES

BRINGING GOOD NEWS TO THE COMMUNITY SINCE 1945

Lost Dreams on Canvas: Annual Gathering Seeks end to Senseless Violence

(From left) Loraine Ballard-Morrill (Radio exec/producer), Rochelle Yates-Whittington (mother of slain youngest son Marcus Yates), Malcolm Yates (her son), Philadelphia Police Commissioner Richard Ross, Anthony Yates (Rochelle's oldest son), Bryan Whittington (Rochelle's husband). Also, present but not pictured, were Tanisha Yates, Myleka Wingate, and Shanice Hayes, younger sisters of slain Marcus Yates.

In a memorable service in the sedate Christ Haven Worship Center sanctuary at 6800 Lindbergh Blvd. December 10, the families and friends, community members and leaders, representatives of religious organization and law enforcement gathered in respectful remembrance of hundreds of persons killed in acts of senseless violence over the past two decades.

In its traditional approach, the Lost Dreams on Canvas organization had girded the sanctuary with dozens of striking portrait paintings of recent and past violence victims.

The event was the 23rd annual Christmas Program conducted by Lost Dreams and featured a special address by guest speaker City Police Commissioner Richard Ross, the presentation of new portraits and

CONTINUES ON PAGE 11

LEWIS C. CASSIDY SCHOOL

MS. JO ANN MANNING, PRIN.
MR. JOHN WISE, ADMIN.ASST.
MRS. SINGLETON
GET SET
1987 - 1988

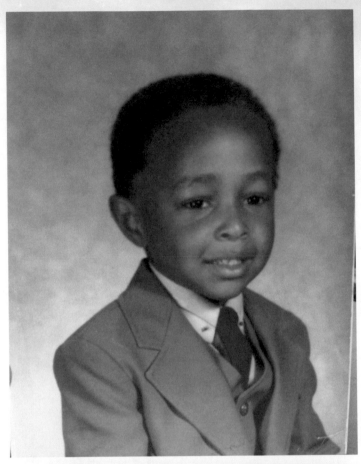

Printed in the United States
by Baker & Taylor Publisher Services